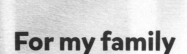

For my family

Copyright © 2019 by Alex Willan
All rights reserved. Published in the United States by Doubleday, an imprint of
Random House Children's Books, a division of Penguin Random House LLC, New York.
Doubleday and the colophon are registered trademarks of Penguin Random House LLC.
Visit us on the Web! rhcbooks.com
Educators and librarians, for a variety of teaching tools, visit us at RHTeachersLibrarians.com
Library of Congress Cataloging-in-Publication Data
Names: Willan, Alex, author, illustrator.
Title: Jasper & Ollie / Alex Willan.
Other titles: Jasper and Ollie
Description: First edition. | New York : Doubleday Books for Young Readers, [2019]
Summary: Jasper, an impatient fox, and Ollie, a slow-moving sloth,
head to the pool on a summer day, each taking their own unique path.
Identifiers: LCCN 2018020615 (print) | LCCN 2018027787 (ebook)
ISBN 978-0-525-64521-4 (hc) | ISBN 978-0-525-64522-1 (glb) | ISBN 978-0-525-64523-8 (ebk)
Subjects: | CYAC: Foxes—Fiction. | Sloths—Fiction. | Individuality—Fiction.
Classification: LCC PZ7.1.W545 (ebook) | LCC PZ7.1.W545 Jas 2019 (print) | DDC [E]—dc23
MANUFACTURED IN CHINA
10 9 8 7 6 5 4 3 2 1
First Edition

JASPER & OLLIE

by Alex Willan

Hey, Ollie, what do you want to do today?

Doubleday Books
for Young Readers

WAIT, I know! Let's go to the pool!

What do you think, Ollie? Should we go to the pool?

Ollie? Hey, Ollie, do you want to go to the pool?

Sounds good to me.

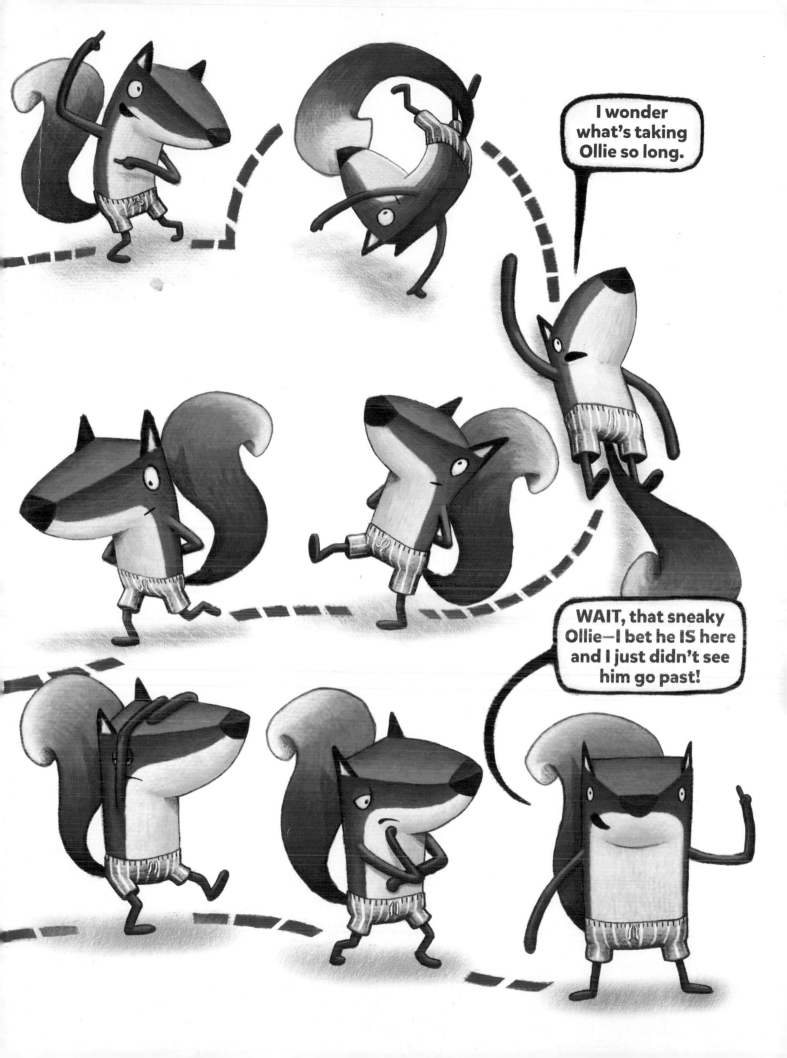

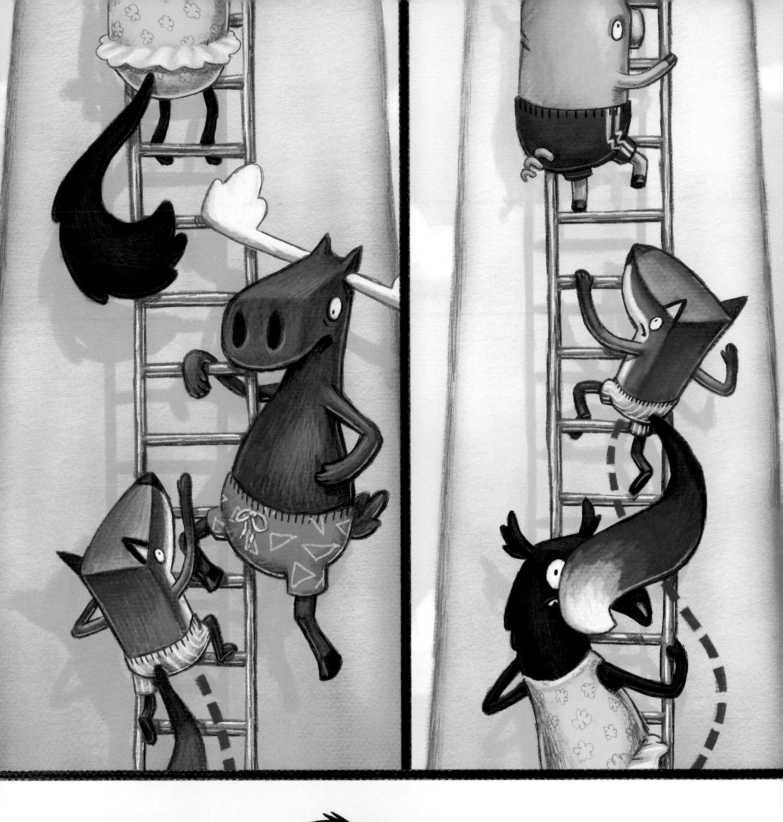

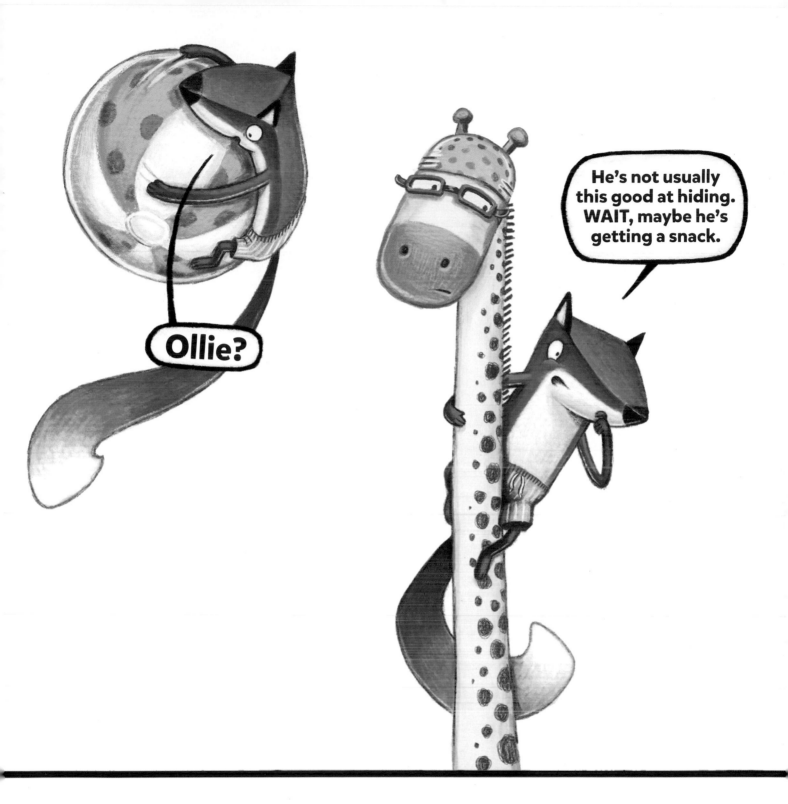

WAIT, of course!
Ollie must already
be in the pool.

Ollie?

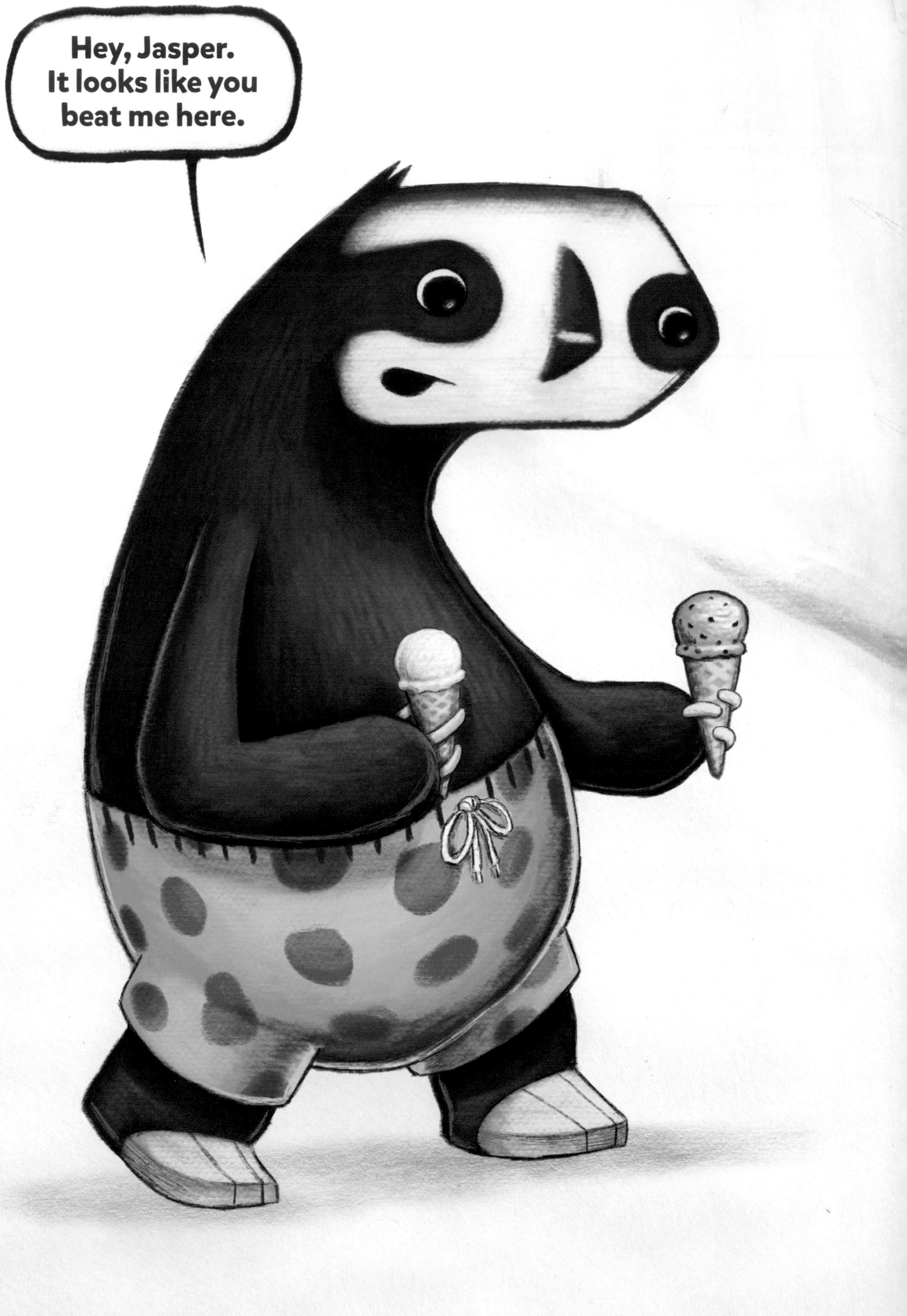
Hey, Jasper. It looks like you beat me here.